J 428.1 NOR
Norton, Patricia J.
Short vowel phonics 4 :
Thad has a job and other tales ;
Digraphs: ch, sh, th, wh /

Short Vowel Phonics 4:
Thad Has a Job
and other tales

Digraphs: ch, sh, th, wh

by: Patricia J. Norton

illustrated by: Sarah E. Cashman

About this book:

<u>Short Vowel Phonics 4</u> is the next book in the Short Vowel Phonics series after book 3. In this book the reader will experience the consonant digraphs:
 ch, sh, th, wh

Two new non-phonetic sight words are added: they, to

Previous non-phonetic sight words: a, as, has, his, is, of, the

Other reading material by the Author:
  Short Vowel Phonics 1
  Short Vowel Phonics 2 a, i
  Short Vowel Phonics 2 o, u, e
  Short Vowel Phonics 3
  Short Vowel Phonics 5
  Short Vowel Phonics Short Stories
  Decodable Alphabet Chart

ISBN: 978-0-9817710-4-5   (lib. bdg.)
[1. Reading - Phonetic method. 2. Reading readiness. 3. Phonics]

Printed and bound in Missouri, U.S.A.

Text font: Pen Time Manuscript

Table of Contents

Notes to Parents and Teachers:

As a child, I loved to read biographies. Not only did I enjoy the story lines, but I learned history and geography in the process. For this reason, in <u>Short Vowel Phonics 4</u>, four of the five stories contain factual details.

Chad is a mini lesson on the country of Chad. The

Mbum people group live in the southern wet area of the country. The name of the people is pronounced as it is spelled.

Shells at Wells' story line takes place in Wells, on

the Gulf of Maine. The staff of the Wells National Estuarine Research Reserve kindly verified the factual details of the area including the flora and fauna that are mentioned in the story.

Thad Has a Job introduces the reader to work of

a search-and-rescue dog. The story takes place in the Black Hills National Forest in South Dakota, which is home to Mount Rushmore. The story mentions an "ash shrub" (*Sorbus scopulina*), also known as the western Mountain ash. It is a deciduous shrub native to South Dakota.

The Land of the Czechs (Cheks) is inspired

by a cultural tradition in the Czech Republic.   A traditional Czech Christmas Eve dinner will have carp. In the week prior to this special meal, fish sellers come into the cities and sell live carp in barrels and tubs. The "chosen" carp is either prepared at the fish stand or taken home, where it swims in the bathtub until it is time to prepare it for the meal. As you can imagine, sometimes children get attached to the fish swimming in their bathtub.

Map 1

Chad

Chapter 1

<u>Chad</u>

Chad is a land in a big land mass. Check Map 1. Chad has wet lands and lands of grass. But much of Chad is sun and sand. Check Map 2.

In Chad, they chat in French.

The land of Chad is rich in clans. Chad has the Mbum clan. They dwell in the wet

Chad

Map 2

sand

grass

west

wet

lands of Chad. The Mbum plant crops.

The land west of Chad has grass, wet lands, and chimps. Chad has grass and wet lands. But Chad has not a chimp.

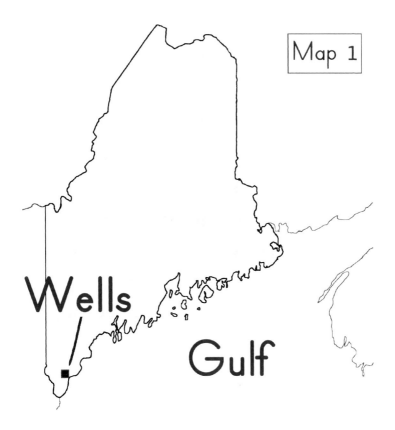

Map 1

Wells

Gulf

Chapter 2

Shells at Wells

Wells is at a gulf. The gulf has fresh wind, sand, rocks and sun. Josh is glad to dwell at the gulf. Josh and his sis, Jen, dwell in Wells. Check Map 1.

1. At Wells

Jen and Josh went shopping in Wells. They got mesh bags at a shop. They went to Wells' dock. At the dock, they got a

lift on a skiff. Check Map 2.

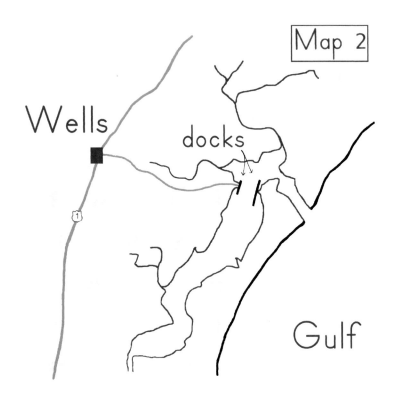

Jen sat in the back of the

skiff. Jen did spot fish

swimming. Jen got a net. "Swish"

went the net. Fish swam in the net. The net went up. The fish went flip and flop in the net.

Jen did drop the net. The fish swam to the gulf.

At the next dock, Jen and Josh left the skiff.

2. At the Gulf

Jen and Josh trek to the gulf. As they trek, they pick up trash. They drop the trash in Jen's mesh bag. They spot ships in the gulf.

The sand has lots of shells. Josh gets a stick and digs in the sand. Josh gets black clam shells. Josh sets the shells in his mesh bag. Jen gets nut shells and a chink shell. A stash of shells ends up in the mesh bag.

Crabs run in the sand. Jen and Josh rush at the crabs. The crabs rush to the rocks and grass.

Josh stops: "Let's not press on. Let's quit and trek back to Wells."

Jen is glad. They trek back to Wells.

3. Back at Wells

Back at Wells, Josh gets the mesh bag of trash. Josh sifts the trash. The cans in the trash Josh has to crush. The cans will end up in a box in the shed. The rest of the trash will end up in the trash can.

Jen gets the bag of shells.

Jen picks up the chink shell. The shell has sand on it. Jen gets a brush. The brush helps get rid of the sand. Jen sets the shell in a box. Jen gets a pen and prints "Chink Shell." Jen sticks it on the box. Jen grabs a nut shell and sets it in a box. Jen has fun.

Jen is glad to dwell in Wells.

chink shell

crab

nut shell

black clam

Chapter 3

Thad Has a Job

Bob Smith is a cop. And Thad is a dog. Thad helps Bob with his job. And cops help us.

Seth is six, and his sis, Beth Ann, is a tot. Mom and Dad plan a big trip. They plan a trip to the Black Hills. Mom and Dad wish to trek in the hills.

1. The Path

In the Black Hills, Mom, Dad,

Seth, and Beth Ann went on a path. Seth and Beth Ann ran up the path. Beth Ann ran fast and hid in an ash shrub. Beth Ann wept and then slept.

Seth ran back to his mom and dad. Seth: "Beth Ann ran up the path and hid."

They had to ask a cop to help them. Bob Smith and Thad went fast to help them.

2. Thad Helps

Bob Smith asks, "Can Thad smell a thing of Beth Ann?"

Seth: "Up the path is Beth Ann's cap. As Beth Ann ran, it fell."

Bob and Thad run up the path. Next to the path is the cap. Thad: "Sniff, sniff, sniff." Thad picks up Beth Ann's scent on the cap. Thad sniffs the path.

Thad tracks Beth Ann's scent. Thad runs up the path with Bob. Thad gets to Beth Ann. Thad sits.

Bob pats Thad. "Grand job, Thad. Grand job!" Bob and Thad bring Beth Ann to Mom and Dad.

Mom and Dad hug Beth Ann. They ask Bob if they can pet Thad. Bob lets them pet Thad.

Thad: "Wag, wag! Thump, thump!"

And that is Thad's job. Thad helps Bob Smith with his job. And Thad helps us.

3. Facts on Scent Sniffing

The skin has skin cells. A skin cell has a scent. The skin sheds skin cells. The cells drift with the wind. They can stick to a plant. They can land on the grass. At the cell's landing spot, a scent is left. A sniffing dog can smell the scent of skin cells.

Beth Ann has on a cap. The cap has shed skin cells of Beth

Ann. The cap has Beth Ann's scent. As Thad sniffs the cap, Thad picks up the scent of Beth Ann's skin cells.

As Beth Ann ran, Beth Ann shed skin cells. Beth Ann left a path of skin cells. To Thad, Beth Ann left a path of scent. Thad did smell the scent. The path of scent led Thad to Beth Ann.

Chapter 4

On a Whim

On a whim, Meg and Liz Whitt get a bat. It is the bat that Dad had in the shed. Meg gets up to bat. Liz has the toss.

The toss.

Meg swings. "Whiz" went the bat.

Miss!

The toss.

Swing. The bat whips the wind.

Miss!

The toss.

Swing. "Whisk" went the bat.

Miss!

Next up to bat is Liz. When Liz has the bat, Liz taps the bat on the grass. Meg has the toss.

The toss.

Liz swings.

Whack! It's a hit!

Crack! The bat has a crack.

Whump! The Whitt's shed

has a dent.

Czech
↓ land

Chapter 5

The Land of the Czechs (Cheks)

1. The Fish Stand

At a Czech (Chek) fish

stand, they sell fresh fish.

Dad has a wish. Dad's wish is to grill fresh fish. Dad gets a glass pot. Dad, Fran, and Max trek to a fish stand.

The fish stand has big tubs. Fresh fish flip and flop in the tubs. Fran and Max pick a cod fish. Dad gets a net. Dad nets the cod. The cod ends up in the glass pot. The fish flaps its gills. The fins "swish" as it swims.

The man at the stand: "That cod is 'a ten' in cash."

Dad hands the glass pot to Fran. Then Dad hands the cash to the man.

Max tells the man, "This is Swish the Fish."

2. At the Flat

They left the fish stand.
When they got to the flat. Max
and Fran went to the bath.
They had to fill the tub. Fran
let the fish swim in the tub.
Fran fed the fish.

Fran and Max went to bed and slept.

When Max gets up, Max checks on Swish the Fish. The fish is swimming in the tub. When Fran gets up, Fran checks the fish. The fish is fed.

At 6, Dad grills the fish. Fran gets a whiff of grilling fish. Fran: "Yum, the smell of grilling fish."

Max: "Yuck, the smell of fish on the grill."

At 7, Dad and Fran sup. Max chugs his milk and has his plum buns. Max has his yam but not the fish.

Max is sad. Max will miss Swish the Fish.